10,000 DRESSES

Story by MARCUS EWERT • Illustrations by REX RAY

SEVEN STORIES

NEW YORK

Text © 2008 by Marcus Ewert
Illustrations © 2008 by Rex Ray

A Seven Stories Press First Edition

Seven Stories Press
140 Watts Street
New York, NY 10013
www.sevenstories.com

In Canada: Publishers Group Canada, 559 College Street, Suite 402, Toronto, ON m6g 1a9

In the UK: Turnaround Publisher Services Ltd., Unit 3, Olympia Trading Estate, Coburg Road,
Wood Green, London n22 6tz

In Australia: Palgrave Macmillan, 15–19 Claremont Street, South Yarra, VIC 3141

Library of Congress Cataloging-in-Publication Data

Ewert, Marcus.
  10,000 dresses / story by Marcus Ewert ; illustrations by Rex Ray. -- 1st
ed.
      p. cm.
  Summary: Bailey longs to wear the beautiful dresses of her dreams but is
ridiculed by her unsympathetic family which rejects her true perception of
herself.
  ISBN 978-1-58322-850-0 (paper over board)
  [1. Identity--Fiction. 2. Transgender people--Fiction. 3.
Self-perception--Fiction. 4. Interpersonal relations--Fiction.] I. Ray,
Rex, ill. II. Title. III. Title: Ten thousand dresses.
  PZ7.E94717Aaj 2008
  [E]--dc22
                                     2008020025
Book design by Rex Ray

Printed in China through Colorcraft Ltd.,Hong Kong

College professors may order examination copies of Seven Stories Press titles for a free
six-month trial period. To order, visit www.sevenstories.com/textbook or send a fax on school
letterhead to (212) 226-1411.

9 8 7 6 5 4 3 2 1

To my parents, with love.
—Marcus

Special thanks to Gent Sturgeon - for Bailey
—Rex

Every night Bailey

dreamed about

dresses

A long staircase led to a red Valentine castle. On each stair was a brand new dress, just waiting to be tried on!

10,000 dresses in all, and each one different!

The first dress was made of crystals.
When **Bailey** slipped the dress on,
the crystals clinked against each other
like millions of tiny bells.
And when sunlight hit the dress just right,
rainbows jumped out!

With all her heart, **Bailey** loved the dress made of
crystals that flashed rainbows in the sun.

When Bailey woke up, she went to find Mother.

Mother was in the kitchen, cutting out coupons.

"Mom, I dreamt about a dress," said Bailey.

"Uh-huh," said her mother.

"A dress made of crystals that flashed rainbows in the sun!"

"Uh-huh."

"And I was wondering if you would buy me a dress like that?"

"Bailey, what are you talking about? You're a **boy**.
Boys don't wear dresses!"

"But...I don't feel like a boy," Bailey said.

"Well, you are one, Bailey, and that's that!
Now go away...and don't mention dresses again!"

Bailey went to her room. Now she would never have a
dress made of crystals that flashed rainbows in the sun.

That night, Bailey walked right past the crystal dress, and went to the second stair.

There was a dress made of lilies and roses! When she slipped it on, she saw that the sleeves were made of honeysuckles!

Bailey picked a few of the blossoms, to taste the little drops of honey.

❋

With all her heart, Bailey loved the dress made of lilies and roses, with honeysuckle sleeves.

Bailey woke up, and went to find Father.

He was in the backyard, pulling up weeds.

"Dad, I dreamt about a dress," Bailey said.

"Uh-huh," said her father.

"A dress made of lilies and roses, with honeysuckle sleeves!"

"Uh-huh."

"And I was wondering if you could grow me a dress like that?"

"Bailey, what are you talking about? You're a **boy**. Boys don't wear dresses!"

"But...I don't feel like a boy," she said.

"Well, you are one, Bailey, and that's that! Now go away, and don't mention dresses again!"

Bailey went to her room. Now she would never have a dress made of lilies and roses, with honeysuckle sleeves.

That night, Bailey walked right past the crystal dress, and the dress made of lilies and roses, and went to the third stair.

❋

There was a dress made of windows. One window showed the **Great Wall of China**, and another, the Pyramids.

With all her heart, Bailey loved the dress made of windows, which showed the **Great Wall of China** and the Pyramids.

Bailey woke up, and went to find her brother.

He was playing soccer with some kids.

"I dreamt about a dress," she told him.

"A dress made of windows, which showed the Great Wall

of China and the Pyramids!"

"You dream about DRESSES, Bailey?

That's gross. You're a **boy**!"

"But..." Bailey said.

"But nothing.

Get out of here, before I kick you!"

Bailey ran and ran. She ran all the way to the end of the block, until she came to a house with a big blue porch.

An older girl was sitting there, with needles and thread and old sheets. "What are you doing?" Bailey asked.

"Making dresses," said the big girl. "But it's really hard. Mine all come out looking the same!"

"Maybe I can help," said Bailey.

Bailey told Laurel, the big girl, about the dress made out of windows, which showed the Great Wall of China and the Pyramids.

"That's awesome!" said Laurel. "But how do we make a dress out of windows?"

"We'll use old mirrors instead," said Bailey.

Together the girls made two new dresses, which were covered with mirrors of all shapes and sizes.

"These dresses don't show us the Great Wall of China, or the Pyramids," said Laurel.

"No," said Bailey, "but they do show us OURSELVES."

"You're the coolest girl I've ever met, Bailey!" said Laurel.

"Hey, do you think you can dream up any MORE dresses?"

Bailey grinned.

"I think I can dream up 10,000!"